DEWDROPS

FROM THE MEMORY LANE

GANESH

Contents

Preface

Dewdrops is a collection close to my heart, inspired by the quiet, often overlooked moments that shape our lives. Each story in this book is a reflection of real-life events, some from my own experiences and others from those I have encountered along the way. These tales are woven from the fabric of everyday life, where the ordinary can suddenly become extraordinary.

As I wrote these stories, I found myself fascinated by the small, seemingly insignificant moments that linger in our memories. Like dewdrops on a leaf, each one is unique, delicate, and reflective of something greater. They capture the essence of fleeting emotions and experiences, holding within them a universe of meaning.

In this first volume of what I hope will be a continuing series, I invite you to join me in exploring these moments. Some stories may evoke a smile, others a tear, and perhaps a few will leave you pondering long after you have turned the last page. My hope is that you will find a bit of your own story within these pages, as I have found mine in writing them.

Throughout the process of bringing this collection to life, I have been fortunate to receive invaluable feedback and testimony from those who read and shared in these stories. Among these voices, even AI has played a role, offering suggestions and reflections that have helped shape the narratives. The collaborative nature of this endeavor, blending human insights with the unique perspective of an AI, has enriched the stories in ways I hadn't anticipated.

This collection is a humble attempt to celebrate the beauty in the everyday and to acknowledge the profound impact of life's subtle nuances. Dewdrops is a tribute to the quiet grace of ordinary life and the extraordinary stories that unfold within it. Thank you for taking the time to share in these moments with me.

1

The Birthday Party!

It was a Sunday afternoon, and it was already 2:00 PM. I was ready and all set for the fifth birthday celebration of Lisa, my sweet niece. My younger sister, Dwitiya, had planned a grand event at Ozone at Marathahalli. She planned the event so early, at 3:00 PM, to pack as many fun events as possible. I had just one hour in hand to reach the venue to be the first person to wish my sweetie, whom I adored the most. If not for my husband, Vikas' Saturday habits of night out and returning home very late, I would have spent time with Lisa from the very morning itself, getting her prepped for the birthday party. I thought to join Dwitya from their home. But Vikas will not turn up if I let him get ready on his own and reach Ozone.

I am getting impatient and annoyed with Vikas. I always hate Saturday nights. Vikas, my lovely husband, goes missing for the whole night on almost all Saturdays. Even though I dislike his absence on Saturdays, I feel happy that he compensates for his absence by giving his whole to me on all Sundays.

I sent my loud and final voice out to Vikas, "Vikas, we will be late to the party. Can you please come out instantly?"

He was still having his shower and yelled back, "Honey! Just a few moments. I will be there with you. It's my promise to you. We will be the first to wish your baby doll."

৷৷৷৷

As I indulged in the refreshing shower, my mind slipped into last evening's fun with old buddies, the partners in crime from my childhood. How much I long to meet with these lunatics the whole week. I cannot imagine a life without this weakness of mine, my friends, and my sweetie, Pratima. They all fill my life with happiness and make every moment meaningful.

Usually, my Saturday ends on a Sunday morning. On most Sundays, I am the first customer to buy milk from the booth that is close to my home. I party all night on Saturday with whisky and end my party with milk. I am blessed with such an understanding wife who feels I deserve a winding down with my friends after a hectic long week. She adores all my friends and respects my space with them once a week. I make the point that we both, Pratima and I, spent an awesome Sunday together. That's all I call happiness, togetherness, and whatnot!

My thoughts were interrupted. Pratima's loud voice demanded that I come out of the shower immediately. I abruptly wound up my shower session and was ready in just a few moments to head out to the party!

We both got into the car, and I promised her I would take her to Ozone in 20 minutes. That is just half the usual commute.

৷৷৷৷

I was lazing and resting in the shade so that my babies would get some energy to play. The breeze from the nearby lake added to the coziness. My babies were sleeping along with me. I feel they are now fully grown and might come out of my womb at any time. I am excited and eagerly waiting for their arrival. I don't know how many are there. This is a suspense I go through every other time I get pregnant. I love this suspense anyway. I was recounting the pleasant moment when we were mating before these kiddos were impregnated into me.

Just then I felt some disturbance—the noise of an object moving at a faster pace. I sensed danger ahead of time. I got up and moved quickly. But the heaviness of the babies inside slowed me a bit. But my intuition told me that it was a survival move. I started running faster. It was too late; the huge object that always terrorizes me just took a lightning turn and hit me on the back. I kept running until I could not run anymore. I realised I could move only a few steps. I was satisfied that it was a hit on the back and that my babies were safe.

I could not move an inch. I stood there moaning out of pain. The pain was getting intense. I looked down. There was blood everywhere. My legs started shivering. I could not stand on my legs. I sat. The blood was oozing out of my body. I felt something totally disconnected in my back. It hurt beyond my bearable limits. I sat down in the bloody pond with the satisfaction that I had saved my babies from the disaster.

I looked at the man sitting under a shelter with the hope that he would understand my pain and help me. I looked at him with agony and deep pain. He walked towards me. Now, I feel confident that he will take care of me. If not me, at least my babies will be saved. My eyes were shutting down. I tried to keep them wide open. They were shutting down again. I finally gave up and put my head down. My eyes drooped. I heard him talking to someone to help me out. I dozed away with hope.

ᐅᐅᐅ

I saw Pratima with a fierce look in her eyes. She was already sitting in the car. She pointed me to her wristwatch and asked me, "Do you know what the time is now? We are not going to make it to the party on time."

I reassured her, "Prati, I will take you there before 2:30 PM. Don't you worry.". I continued, "You know my driving skills. My honks have the magic to keep people off the road. My honks are special. You know that." I winked at her. She blushed instantly. "Stop your naughty wink. Let's get going right away. I know your talent." She continued blushing.

I got my beast to life, and with all my forces, I brought him to a loud roar and instantly hit the road at my passionate speed. I honked all the way and kept every other slow-moving scooter and car off the road. I told Prati, "These folks on the road do not have any urgency. Look at the speed at which they are going, occupying the road, and denying paths to others. They are on the road as though they never want to reach their home." She chuckled. I kept my eyes on the road, with one hand on the steering wheel and the other on the horn. "Only honking helps on the road," I said. She acknowledged and replied, "Someone must teach them to drive faster. Look at the way they are driving in a straight line, one after the other. I guess they don't know the purpose of horns. It looks like all the morons have taken to the road all at once." I nodded back to her with a smile.

In no time, we reached the Ozone Resorts. It was still 2:25 PM. As we took the narrow lane that led to the resort, I looked at Prati and asked her to check her watch. She looked at me with pride and said, "I know, darling, you will make it. You saved me from the embarrassment of being late to my darling Lisa's birthday celebration.

I took a swift turn, the last turn to reach the resort. I saw a dog lying down and lazing on the road. She did not seem to even bother the speeding car coming towards her. She was walking at a sweet pace of her own. I honked at her. I would have almost run over her. Thankfully, it just hit her back. Pratima looked at me and said with disappointment, "These stray dogs are really a menace. Thankfully, you saved her life." She gave a proud glance at me. When I hit the brake, it was exactly 2:30 PM. The moment she got out of the car, Pratima hugged me and thanked me for getting her on time. As she paced towards the party hall, she noticed that Dwitiya, along with Lisa and her husband, Sunil, had just arrived. Perfect timing.

ϸϸϸ

I saw the speeding car that hit the pregnant Betsy on her back and rushed at the same speed without even stopping to look at what had just happened. Betsy tried to run. But her body, with puppies inside, did not support the speed. I could sense that she was trying to make a quick move. Just before she could react to the danger coming her way, the car hit her in the back. She was howling and running as fast as she could in search of a safe place. She made her best effort. But she finally succumbed to the pain. She was profusely bleeding and stopped in front of my shop. I felt she was feeling dizzy due to pain and the loss of blood from her body. I got worried about her condition and her unborn puppies. She looked up at me with immense pain. She kept looking at me for some time. The painful look conveyed just one thing: "Please save my kids."

Just then, I saw Krishna walking towards my shop. He passed by Betsy, totally puzzled and trying to assimilate her painful condition. He came near me, looked back at Betsy once again, and locked my eyes.

☙☙☙

I parked my scooter near Raghu's shop and walked towards the shop. Just then I noticed a female dog sitting in an awkward position, and it was moaning with utter pain. There was blood surrounding her. Her stomach was bulging. She must be pregnant, holding almost full-grown puppies, waiting to jump out of her womb, and eager to see a new world.

As I approached the shop, I turned back and was not able to divert my eyes away from the groaning female dog. Raghu mentioned that a speeding car that took an abrupt turn towards Ozone Resort hit her on her back while she was trying to move away. She was resting on the left bank of the street when this speeding car hit her harshly and got away as though nothing unusual had occurred.

Raghu and I shared the pity state of the female dog and the fate of her unborn puppies. We were both puzzled as to what to do now. Raghu asked me if I could do something to save her.

I nodded with affirmation. Yes. Let's do something about this. I was getting enraged at the irresponsible driver of the car. How can someone be so insensible while driving through narrow streets? That too, at the turn. I googled for animal help on my mobile phone. The first help I found was the CUPA helpline number.

I dialled the number, and a female voice answered on the other side. Her voice cancelled my sceptical thought about whether someone would be there to answer as it was a Sunday afternoon. I described the situation to the lady and asked if she could help the injured dog. My heart felt deep pain when I was talking over the phone. I could sense the same emotions in Raghu. I looked at him and could sense a calmness dawning upon him as he sensed some help was on the way.

The lady from CUPA asked me to send a picture of the injured dog. I clicked photos instantly and sent them to her WhatsApp number that she shared with me. She called back in a few minutes and informed me that an ambulance was about to leave to pick up the injured dog. She also said that looking at the condition of the dog, it looks like her lower back bone is fractured, and that is the reason she is not able to move. I shared my location with her. She mentioned it might take around 30 to 45 minutes for the ambulance to reach. I asked Raghu to call me once the ambulance reached here and left for home. I assured him I would be there within two minutes of his call, as I live close by. I waited at home for Raghu's call. My phone rang after exactly forty minutes. I rushed there immediately.

The rescuers were carefully lifting the dog and placing her in the ambulance. I called back the lady at CUPA once again to inform her about the arrival of help and thanked her for the rapid action. She asked if I could donate some money to CUPA to take care of the ambulance expenses. She told me any small amount, as small as 500 rupees, would suffice. Raghu jumped in instantly with a contribution of 500 rupees from his side. I informed the lady that we were donating 1000 rupees. She thanked me and told me she would call me back once the veterinary doctor inspected the dog.

ﮞﮞﮞ

I reached Raghu's shop for my usual feeding of all the homeless dogs that resided near the lake close to Raghu's petty shop. As I was feeding, I did not find Betsy, the female dog for whom I take special care, as she was in her final leg of pregnancy. I asked Raghu, "Where is Betsy? I can't see her around." Raghu narrated to me what just happened with Betsy. I became overtly emotional. I felt very sad for Betsy. I told Raghu that she was due for delivery any time in the next three or four days. I will bear all the expenses to save her. Raghu told me Krishna; his regular customer is in constant touch with the CUPA people. I told Raghu, "Please ask Krishna to convey this to the doctor in CUPA to proceed with the treatment to save Betsy." Raghu called this person Krishna immediately and conveyed my message. I felt some kind of gratitude toward Krishna, whom I have never met.

🐾🐾🐾

I received a call from Dr. Pramod, the veterinary doctor at CUPA. "Mr. Krishna, our saviors have just arrived here with the injured dog you helped transport to us. I inspected her situation. Her lower back bone is fractured. The possibility of survival with a fracture in this part of the body is the bare minimum, and it is also futile to restructure the fracture. Such a fracture has an immense effect on the rectum. She will not be able to pass motion owing to the pain. Moreover, she is pregnant, and she cannot even push the baby out due to the fracture coupled with pain. The puppies will die inside if we do not act immediately.

I said, "Doctor, there is a gentleman who is willing to bear the whole expense of her treatment."

"Mr. Krishna, this is not about money. This is about the pain she will endure throughout her whole life. Even if I save her, she will not be able to pass motion and will die in the next few days. Rather, I suggest we give her a peaceful death and, at the same time, save her kids. Hence, I require your permission to perform 'mercy killing' on her. Since you are the person who sent her to us, we only need your consent to proceed. This is the formality we need to follow. We cannot take further steps without your approval. I, as a doctor, though I have seen many cases, have never come across such a condition. She is dying of pain every moment of her life. I can see in her eyes; she is begging for death."

I looked at Raghu, totally puzzled. Raghu was looking more puzzled than I was. I took a deep breath, bringing up courage. "Doctor, if this is the only option left with us, please proceed." I can feel Raghu's eyes getting wet, and the same was happening inside me as well.

We both murmured, "Rest in peace, Betsy."

ᭉᭉᭉ

It was a wonderful party today. My loving niece had a great time with all the attention and gifts she received from the guests. I was feeling so content seeing my pretty girl, adding one more year of happiness to our lives. I asked Vikas, "Do you want me to drive back home? You have downed a few more pegs than me. Let me drive today, and you sit relaxed." He replied, "Look at you. You look more dizzied than me. With the josh inside, now I can take you home in half the time it took for us to reach here." He laughed. I laughed back and spoke. "As you please, my honey." I feel more love for him when I am dizzy after a few rounds of my favourite scotch, Black Dog. "Yes. Let's reach home quickly. I am getting hungry. I am going to feast on you. I am going to eat you out the whole night." I kissed him on his cheek and instantly pushed him away as he turned towards my lips to steal a quick smooch. I said, "Hold on for 10 minutes, honey."

I placed my hand on his groin and pressed there with vigor, only to feel that he was hard there already. Vikas thrust his beast with a roar and with double the vigor. I felt we would get back home in five minutes.

As we came out of the resort, my eyes hovered over the place where the dog was about to spoil our party mood. It was not to be seen around.

I turned to Vikas. He was also looking for the same dog, and he uttered, "Street dogs."

2
The Book Worm

As the train jolted into motion from Swami Vivekananda Metro Station, Manoj sank into a comfortable seat in the compartment. Beside him sat his friend Maya, her eyes scanning the crowd with a casual look on her face.

Manoj retrieved a book from his Lavie Sport backpack. He flipped open the book to where he had left off and started reading. Maya peeped into the title of the book. She did not understand a single word printed on the cover.

"Another day, another book, huh?" Maya teased, nodding towards the book in Manoj's hand. "Don't you ever get tired of living in the past? We are in the digital age now, Manoj. Time to join the rest of us."

Manoj returned a smile to Maya's gentle ribbing. "Books are my sanctuary, Maya," he replied, adjusting the position of the bag below his seat. "They are windows to the worlds, portals to new ideas. Why trade that for the shallow distractions of technology?"

Maya shook her head, a playful glint in her eyes. "Oh, come on, Manoj," she nagged. "You make it sound like books are some kind of sacred relic. We have the internet now, you know. With just a few clicks, I can access more information than you could find in a hundred books."

Manoj raised an eyebrow. "Information, Maya, is not the same as knowledge," he countered, holding up his book. "Sure, you can find facts and figures online, but can you find wisdom? Can you find the profound insights and timeless truths that only a splendid work of literature can offer?"

Maya sighed, rolling her eyes in mock exasperation. "You're such a romantic, Manoj," she teased. "But I'll humour you. Tell me, what profound insights have you found in that little book of yours?"

"Well," he began, his voice filled with enthusiasm, "This book, named "Aram" by Jeyamohan, for example, is a collection of short stories. Each one offers a glimpse into the lives of ordinary people who lived extraordinary lives, and there is a wealth of wisdom they left through their lives."

Maya leaned back in her seat, intrigued by Manoj's explanation. "Such as?" she prompted, her curiosity piqued.

"Such as this short story named 'Yanai Doctor' which means 'The Elephant Doctor', I'm reading now," Manoj continued, his eyes lighting up with excitement. "It's about a veterinary doctor who lived in the deepest forest of Mudhumalai. He is specialised in treating wild elephants. He was fondly called as 'The Elephant Doctor'. The elephants remember him so well that they walk more than 300 kilometres to remove the beer bottles that is struck in their foot. The same beer bottles that some of the so called urban grown-ups throw thoughtlessly in the forests."

Maya listened intently, her interest growing with each word. "That does sound fascinating," she admitted, leaning forward to get a better look at the book in Manoj's hands. "But can't you find stories like that online?"

"Perhaps," Manoj conceded, "but there's something special about holding a book in your hands, about turning the pages and immersing yourself in the story. It's a tactile experience, a connection to the past, present, and future all at once."

Manoj continued, "Maya, have a glance around the carriage of this train and tell me what you observed". Maya glanced around and noticed a sea of faces illuminated by the soft glow of their mobile screens. Each passenger was engrossed in their own digital realm, lost in a maze of videos, and sifting the apps that popped up notifications. With a pang of sadness, Manoj told, "Look at the cacophony of modern life. Everyone is lost in the world of pure indulgent in visual media that has the power of making you dumb eventually. The beauty of literature is underrated here."

As they were immersed in deep conversation, the train arrived at Cubbon Park station. They alighted and walked towards the lush greenery of the Cubbon Park. The warmth of the afternoon sun was filtering through the canopy of trees above. The sights and sounds of nature rendered a soothing comfort and they both fell into a comfortable silence, drifting into their own thoughts.

Manoj found a cozy seat and sat down. Maya continued with strolling around the park. Manoj grabbed his book once again after spending some time assimilating the beauty of the nature.

Maya returned to Manoj after fifteen minutes of walk through the park and found him deeply lost into the book once again. She sat beside him in silence and closed her eyes and was prepping herself for a deep meditation.

As she closed her eyes to plunge into the mystic world, her mind was still ringing around the life of the elephant doctor. She felt a deep gratitude to the selfless doctor whom she was not even aware of just a few moments back. She opened her eyes abruptly and turned to Manoj, who was still absorbed in the story with no awareness of the surroundings.

Maya gently tapped on Manoj's shoulder. He lifted his eyes from the book and turned to her with a question mark in his face. Maya spoke with a spark in her eyes, "Manoj, would you mind reading this story loud and translate it for me". Manoj replied, "Oh sure! With all the pleasure. But Maya you won't understand the original prose. It's written in Tamil." Maya replied with curiosity, "I am curious to learn more about the elephant doctor and at the same time to know how another language sounds like. How different it would sound from my mother tongue Kannada". Manoj's eyes gleamed with a spark, "That sounds interesting, Maya. I would love to read the whole story for you and translate as well. That's indeed a great honour to read a story to my bestie".

Manoj read the story aloud, pausing after each paragraph to explain it to Maya. She was captivated by the narration and moved by the doctor's selfless dedication to the elephants throughout his life. The story vividly portrayed the deep friendship between the wild animals of Mudhmalai forest and the doctor. Maya gained a deeper understanding of greatness of elephants through the doctor's eyes.

After Manoj finished reading the final line, Maya's eyes brimmed with tears. She made no effort to wipe them away, remaining seated in stunned silence. Beside her, Manoj patiently waited for her to regain composure, knowing the story had stirred deep emotions within her.

Maya eventually regained her composure and dabbed her tears with a napkin from her duffle bag. She shyly smiled at Manoj, expressing immense gratitude for sharing such an inspiring story with her. "Sorry, I got too emotional," she said. "This is truly touching. Thank you for introducing me to a legend who lived in our time and led such a remarkable life."

"That's very true Maya", Manoj reciprocated and continued, "Now you see what is there in these books I read. These books are not mere papers that you would like to turn over. These papers exhibit many wisdoms that has the power to change our lives." Maya acknowledged, "Tell me more about books and what makes people, including me, not motivated to read".

Manoj looked deep into her eyes, "Maya, if I must tell you about what it takes to cultivate a habit of reading, it cannot be explained in one or two sentences. It's going to be a painful long lecture. That will certainly test your patience, a trait unique to reader.", he said with a teasing tone.

"Hey, that's fine. I am all ears to hear that. Especially, after hearing to the doctor's story I feel motivated to read more. I am all set to go through your long session to kindle my motivation. Get going buddy!"

"Maya, reading books is something most of us stop the very moment we complete our academics. In fact, we are more than eager to get rid of the books that had been nagging us ever since we stepped into the school.

I have asked many fresh grads, which book they read lastly. The answer is most of the time the textbooks during their college or a few enthusiastic ones talk about a popular self-development book. The next question I ask is how valuable they found the book to be, the response is, they are yet to start reading the book.

You must have noticed that there is a steep decline amongst youngsters as well as the grown up in reading of books. The mobile phones have largely added to the transition. The common answer from someone who does not read books will usually be like, 'I am a very practical person and believe in learning by experiencing on my own. Reading book is a hobby of lazy folks, the book worms who don't want to raise up from their couch and explore the life in its fullest form'."

Maya and Manoj raised and started strolling along the walking trail. Manoj continued, "When you take a deep dive into their reasons to find out what could be the possible truth, we get not one but multiple reasons. The first one, I personally feel is their lack of appetite to read through a book. It requires effort from an individual to read, assimilate and finally complete a book. That's the reason videos are gaining popularity these days. Videos get over even you don't watch. Whereas you need to read through the book to complete it"

Maya nodded with an acknowledgement, "Manoj, this sounds like an interesting analysis you have made over the years of your observations. I am sure, you have more to share. I'm really enjoying our conversation as we stroll around. I can tell this is going to get intense. Why don't we head to the India Coffee House and complement our wonderful conversation with a wonderful aromatic coffee?"

"That's a lovely idea, Maya. Coffees and conversations are a perfect blend. Let's go there."

As they started walking towards IHC, Manoj continued, "The next reason is lack of imagination. To read a book, be it fiction or non-fiction one needs to exercise imagination and create a space for the contents in their head. Else, a reader cannot understand a single word that is written in it.

Also, many people reject a book for those words that they do not understand and find these does not make any sense to them. They move away from the book because they struggle to understand its contents, mainly due to their limited vocabulary. The truth is, we develop a good vocabulary only by reading lot of books and not by avoiding it."

Manoj slipped into a deep thought as his mind was running through the merits of reading books. Maya realised that he is composing his thoughts and walked in silence. Soon they reached the legendary India Coffee House and ordered for a coffee. As they were waiting for the coffee to arrive, Manoj started to enumerate the many merits that a book holds besides the reasons he narrated about why people don't want to read. He remarked that someone could talk themselves out of reading for their entire life, not even realizing what they're missing out on. He mentioned, "The loss of not reading is farfetched than one might not be even aware of what they are missing. This ignorance is certainly not a bliss." Maya smiled with an understanding of his last statement.

Manoj continued after he took a sip of the coffee, "Let us look at a few interesting factors that a book has got to offer. A book has got the power to change the thought process of the reader. A reader is reborn with every book they finish. The famous quote by Cassandra Clare confirms this, "One must always be careful of books, and what is inside them, for words have the power to change us."

"Unlike videos, each reader has the liberty to imagine in their own way. Videos are the imagination of its creator. A book though created by a person can have several dimensions according to each reader. So, a book takes many avatars as per the number of people who read it. Reading books will kindle one's imagination to the greater level. With just one book one can create so many imaginations. Reading many books will invariably make the reader a creator."

"It is not possible in one life to learn everything through one's own experience. At times, these experience render awfully expensive. Someone somewhere has gone through a similar experience before you. We just need to read through their experience. We need not restrict to one person's experience but invest on reading lots of such experiences. These experiences are written as a book by many people. We just need to read through the book and implement what suits us. So, the belief of practical experience only gets better as we have sufficient inputs with us to act upon any given situation prudently".

"Reading a book is like having a virtual chat with the author. Having a coffee in hand with the book will add flavour of having a coffee with the author. Countless geniuses have lived and continue to live on this Earth. It is nearly impossible for them to reach everyone or everyone to reach them. Fortunately, many of these brilliant minds have documented their thoughts, inventions, and imaginations in books for the benefit of mankind. The simplest way to connect with these geniuses is - Just grab a coffee and a book and they are with you talking to you. A reader is always blessed to meet a genius every time he or she picks a book and completes reading it too".

"Wow! This is profound Manoj. Having a coffee with the author. I am having a coffee with a genius who has all the concoction to be an author. I might very soon have a coffee with a real author", Maya commented.

Manoj commented back quickly, "I don't know about that yet Maya. But I can see in your eyes that an author already taking birth inside you".

He continued, "Every book we read leaves so many experiences in us. It is like living many lives in this one life we have. Not reading a book is living a mundane life. Books adds so many flavours and experience that one gets only through reading."

They raised to leave the ICH and Manoj stated, "Maya, do you still have a doubt about the vast benefits of reading book? I can keep adding benefits that could amount to become a book by itself that you may want to read." Maya replied, "Look here. The author is already born". Manoj laughed. They continued their talk as they walked through pavement of MG Road.

"Let me conclude with a final thought. Maya, when you are in need of an advice whom do you reach out first? You reach out to a friend right? A friend will give you solution to a limit of his knowledge and at times may not be accessible immediately due to many constraints. A book is such a friend, always accessible and can provide a wise solution. On a lonely day when there is no one around what can be a good company other than a book. A book is the best comparison to the famous quote, 'A friend in need is a friend indeed'".

"Only a strong willed person can complete a book! Unlike a pie, you can always have a book and read it too!"

"So Maya, for your next journey, go grab a book – your best companion ever..." As Manoj concluded, Maya stopped walking, spelled a secret smile. He asked her what was brewing. She told with a mischievous look, "MANOJ! I am grabbing a book right here and now". Manoj asked how.

She held his index finger into her hand and pointed at a board above him. On the board, was written in bold letters -
HIGGINBOTHOMS

3

The Uncommon People

Malar felt accomplished as she wrapped up her work ahead of schedule. She had a few hours to kill in the Pearl City before her flight. Despite her desire to explore the city, the limited time remaining, compelled her to head to the airport. Spending the addtional two hours in reading at the airport lounge sounded like the perfect way to fill the gap.

Upon arriving at the airport around 5:00 PM for her 8:00 PM flight, she joined a bustling crowd of passengers navigating their way to various gates. Despite the chaos, an air of solemnity encompassed the place, with each person preoccupied in their own worlds.

Malar found a quieter spot with a view of her gate and settled down with a book. She immersed herself into the book at the same time kept an eye on the ticking time.

However, the peace was soon disrupted by an announcement of her flight's delay and a gate change due to the airline staff needing to clear the designated counter for another departure. Early birds who had positioned themselves an hour ahead of time at the gate were now troubled to lose their ace position to enter the gate first.

The disappointment quickly turned to agitation as passengers jostled to secure their positions at the new counter. Another announcement stating an additional hour's delay aggravated the situation. The crowd, now agitated, abandoned the entry gate, and rushed towards the customer service desk.

There emerged a natural leader of the crowd, representing the frustrated passengers and demanding the reasons for the delay and the reason for the shift of entry gate. A young woman at the desk, trying to cope with the situation, faced the leader's persistent questioning, amplified by the support of the crowd.

Malar had no desire to join the fray. Delays were an occasional inconvenience beyond the control of airlines and airports. Nonetheless, she felt that there was always room for improvement in service levels. Meanwhile, the mob berated everything under the sky ranging from the airline and airport authorities to the government and even the sky itself.

As the agitation continued, Malar noticed a movement out of the corner of her right eye. A security guard in uniform was approaching the gate from the other side of the gate. Calmly, she returned her book to her bag, straightened her clothes, and stood up. She walked with a sense of detachment, as though she had no connection to the commotion around her.

She entered the deserted path leading to the gate, while the mob continued their verbal assault at the Help Desk representative, who valiantly attempted to provide answers to their questions. Malar admired the way this lady managed the situation effectively.

The security guard unlocked the barrier chain at the entry gate to allow passengers to enter for onboarding.

Malar reached the gate to be the first to enter inside for the onboarding.

This caught the attention of a few agitated passengers, and the leader once again took charge, demanding to know how this young girl was allowed ahead of them. He further demanded the young lady at Help Desk, "Is she a VIP or a celebrity?", he added, "Is there not a place in this country for common people?"

Amused, the lady responded, "Sir, she is neither a VIP nor a celebrity."

Puzzled, the leader inquired further, "Then why is she being allowed inside while we have been waiting in line for so long?"

She replied with a smile, "Sir, you were queuing up at the Help Desk counter instead of the entry gate. The young lady over there simply positioned herself at a perfect moment at the perfect space."

Just as Malar was about to step in, she noticed an elderly couple approaching from behind. The man was in a wheelchair, and a woman accompanied him. They were both gently escorted by airport staff toward the entry.

Malar graciously stepped aside, allowing the elderly couple to enter.

The young lady at the desk concluded, "She, too, is one among the common people, but with common sense."

4

The Red Box

Vinod carefully dropped the letter into the red box, addressed to an old friend Girish whom he hadn't seen in many years. The box swallowed his letter, maintaining its ever-innocent appearance.

Sanjay, who was standing a few feet away, adjusting his cap with a grizzled hand, nodded towards the red box. "These boxes, they've been our link to home, haven't they? When we were out there in faraway towns and battle fields across the nation, letters were all we had to keep us grounded."

Vinod, nodding in agreement, recalled their time in service. "Absolutely, Sanjay. Letters were our lifeline amidst the near nomadic times during our deployments in the remote places."

Rajesh, leaning against the nearby wall, smiled expressively. "They held our joys, our sorrows, and every bit of news that mattered from back home. Nothing beat the feeling of receiving one after a long mission."

Sanjay's gaze turned reflective. "I remember the anticipation every time we walked past the pigeonholes placed outside our mess hall. Hoping for a letter, hoping to hear good news."

Vinod, lost in thought, stared at the red box. "It's strange, isn't it? How these boxes carried so much of our lives. They were more than just containers of letters."

Rajesh nodded sagely. "They were a lifeline, a connection to everything we held dear. Even now, seeing one takes me back to those days."

Vinod stood there, motionless, unable to move away from this red box that had just swallowed his emotions and the precious message to his old comrade. It felt strange. He felt a sense of loss as the letter mysteriously sunk into the heap of others.

Lost in thought, he suddenly realized why he was fixated on the Red Box. "I was searching for a 'SEND' button," Vinod muttered to himself. "A post box having a send button?"

Sanjay chuckled softly. "Ah, the times have indeed changed. From waiting weeks for a letter to instant communication."

Vinod nodded, a hint of nostalgia in his voice. "Yes, but there was something special about those days. The anticipation, the uncertainty..."

Rajesh chimed in; his voice nostalgic. "Soon, this adorable Red Box would be extinct, permanently removed from our lives."

They all echoed in unison, "The good old Red Box, it will live forever in our memories."

Suddenly, Vinod felt a haunting gaze locked onto him, brimming with deep sorrow. He turned around and saw everyone around him smiling. Where was this sorrowful and heartbreaking gaze coming from?

His eyes turned towards the red box.

5

Integrity — Comes in Different Sizes

The midday sun beat down relentlessly on the crowded market square as Suresh made his way through the throngs of shoppers. Amidst the bustling chaos, a flash of lavender caught his eyes – a neatly folded one hundred rupee note lying innocuously on the pavement. He hesitated for a split second, then stooped to retrieve it, his fingers brushing against the rough texture of the note. As he unfolded the note, there he was - Mahatma Gandhi, gazing back at him with an encompassing smile.

Without a second thought, he held up the note to see if it belonged to anyone nearby, feeling a surge of pride in his own goodness washing over him. There were good-hearted people out there too. Everyone checked their own wallets and purses, shrugged, and departed, acknowledging that the money did not belong to them.

He held the money in his hand, uncertain of the next step, and stood there quietly, hoping the rightful owner would return to claim it. With no luck, he carefully stowed the money in a separate pocket, keeping it apart from his own.

Just then, Suresh then remembered his lunch meeting with his friend Pramod. He hurried to catch up with him at a bustling eatery where they planned to enjoy hot Hyderabadi dum biriyani. As they savoured their meal, Suresh couldn't hold back sharing his find.

"So, Pramod, guess what I stumbled upon today," Suresh began, glancing at Pramod with a knowing smile.

Pramod raised an eyebrow, curious. "What's the story?"

Suresh recounted the incident, from spotting the money to the ethical dilemma it posed. "I didn't know what to do at first. Should I keep it or...?"

Pramod listened intently, nodding thoughtfully. "It's like a test of integrity found you in the middle of the market."

"Yeah," Suresh agreed, leaning in. "It made me wonder, what if it were a larger amount? Would I react the same way? Would others?"

Pramod considered the question, "Integrity doesn't change with the size of the test. It's about what feels right, no matter the circumstances."

Suresh nodded slowly, absorbing Pramod's words. "You're right. It's not about the size of the test, but how we choose to face it."

"Well said," Pramod nodded approvingly. "Remember, integrity isn't about the size of the challenge, but the extent of our response."

As they finished their meal, Suresh felt a sense of clarity and peace. The incident had sparked a meaningful conversation and left him reflecting on the varying sizes of integrity in everyday life.

"Well!" Suresh mused, breaking the silence. "The story ends here since the test of integrity came in a smaller size. But what if integrity comes in diverse sizes – like clothes or footwear?"

Pramod smiled knowingly. "Indeed. What if you had found a lakh or a crore? Would your reaction be the same? Would others have responded similarly, or would my advice have changed?"

Suresh pondered these questions, his mind racing with possibilities. "Let us rewind and think about it..."

6

Zero the Hero

Me: I am unhappy and disappointed. My hard work does not result in success.

God: Your hard work is nothing but a zero.

Me: Please God! Do not hurt me. I work harder every day to achieve my goals. I still do not see success anywhere nearby.

God: You work harder? Well! That is still a zero.

Me: But God I was taught hard work and dedication is the key to success.

God: Your hard work is a zero and your dedication is a zero too.

Me: God! Please have mercy on me. I hope you will at least agree to this – 90% perspiration and 10% luck will make you a successful person.

God: Your Perspiration? That too is a zero.

Me: So, you say all I learnt is false. I beg you. Will you also deny this – Your attitude will take you to altitude.

God: Your attitude. (ponders) Yes. That too is a zero.

Me: Now, I am confused. I do not know what is right for me. I am losing hope. I am losing my confidence. I am losing trust in everything. Why do you do this to me? Don't

I deserve success? Why do you punish me? WHY ME?

God: I have given you all the ability, so that you could work hard with more dedication.

Me: But you said these are zeros

God: Yes. These are zeros. You keep adding these zeros to your life every day. Someday, I will place '1' in front of your zeros. Your success will lie in the number of zeros you have added to your life. So, stop worrying about 'success' now. I anyway will give you that. Start adding zeros. The greater the better!

7
The Tensed Ten Minutes

The party was about to over after a sumptuous lunch. Prabhakar stretching contentedly after the big lunch in the backyard, "The food was amazing, and it's so nice seeing everyone before the winter really sets in." The backyard of the family quarters was filled with laughter and chatter, with everyone enjoying one last day together before the cold grip of the Himalayan winter took over Meghalaya.

"Yeah, it's already getting chilly. The nights are starting to outlast the days," another added, glancing at the sky. "In a few days, it's going to be short days and long nights. I always forget how quickly it changes."

"Tell me about it," Abdul chimed in. "Most families are already planning to head back to their hometowns with the kids. It's like an annual migration," Prabhakar, Nagaraj and Parashuram chuckled in unison. "We won't get to see them again until summer. This party really feels like a last bravo before everyone heads out."

On the other end, Nandini and Priya were in deep discussion explaining Parveena about this annual unavoidable ceremony. "Most families head home around this time," Nandini added, glancing around at the group.

"No one wants to be stuck here with the kids when it's freezing. We all come back to Shillong once summer is in full swing." "Exactly," Priya smiled. "Everyone's packing up to spend a few months with their parents."

"But not you guys, right?" Parashuram asked, turning to Abdul. "You're staying?"

Abdul had come to Shillong with his wife, Parveena, and their daughter, Naseeba, just a few months ago.

"Yeah, we decided to stick around," Abdul replied looking at Parveena who turned from her conversation with Nandini and Priya and nodded in agreement. "It's our first time having our own space since we got married. We wanted to experience it fully.

Parveena smiled, "It's exciting, actually. A little daunting, but exciting. We want to make the most of it, even with the cold coming."

"That's brave of you," one of the friends said, grinning. "It can get pretty cold, but it's a unique experience for sure. Plus, it's a great chance to really settle in and make this place feel like home."

"Yeah," Parveena added, smiling. "We've had some great advice and tips from everyone, so we feel ready. It's exciting, in a way, to see how we'll manage."

As the laughter continued, Parushuram, who had been caring on little Naseeba, suddenly noticed something was terribly awry. Naseeba, nestled in Abdul's arms, had grown alarmingly pale.

"Abdul, she's shivering badly, and her face... it doesn't look right," Parushuram's voice was urgent, breaking through the festive buzz. His warning quickly caught the attention of the entire group. Laughter faded, replaced by a collective hush that turned the atmosphere from light-hearted to grim.

Parveena's eyes widened with panic, her composure failing her as tears welled up, threatening to spill over. "Abdul, what's happening with her?" she cried, her voice trembling.

The air was thick with tension. Amidst the chaos, one clear command echoed from every corner: "RUN, ABDUL, RUN!"

Without hesitation, Abdul clutched Naseeba tightly to his chest, his heart pounding. He leaped off the porch and dashed down the hill. As he glanced around, he saw Nagaraj, swoop in and pick up Parveena on his bike. "Go, Abdul bhai!" Nagaraj shouted, urgency lacing his voice. "You'll get to the hospital before us. Don't wait!"

With the gravity of the situation propelling him, Abdul raced down the hill, his steps echoing against the stone path. He hurdled over the uneven steps, each jump taking him closer to the clinic. As he approached, he risked a quick glance back up the winding road. The motorcycle was still a distant sight.

As Abdul burst into the clinic, his heart racing with a mix of hope and dread, he was relieved to see Rajesh, the Clinic Assistant, already waiting at the reception. Rajesh had been alerted by the sight of Abdul running down the hill with the baby in his arms.

"I saw someone racing down with a baby and knew something was wrong," Rajesh said, his face a mask of concern. He guided Abdul to an examination bed with calm efficiency. "Lay her down here," he instructed.

Abdul gently placed Naseeba on the bed, his breath hitching as he watched her. To his utter disbelief, Naseeba, instead of appearing distressed, greeted him with her familiar, endearing smile. Both Abdul and Rajesh stared at her in confusion.

Rajesh examined Naseeba thoroughly, his brow furrowed in concentration. "She seems perfectly fine," he finally said, his tone filled with relief. "There's a bit of phlegm, which is normal for kids at this time of year. It seems her high fever must have caused a brief fit, but the cool air from the descent likely helped lower her temperature quickly."

Just then, Parveena arrived, her face etched with worry and anxiety. Her heart melted at the sight of Naseeba reaching out with a smile, her tiny hands lifted toward her mother. "Ammi!" Naseeba cooed, her distress evaporating in the comfort of her mother's embrace.

The traumatic ten minutes now seemed like a distant memory as Naseeba's smile and Parveena's tearful joy filled the room. The ordeal had been intense, but the quick action and the cool breeze had worked wonders, turning a moment of panic into a story of unexpected relief.

8
The Ticking Time Bomb

❦

Kavya and Mark walked into the dimly lit coffee shop. As they entered they noticed the coffee shop was almost empty. Kavya felt this is the perfect place and moment for Mark and her. They both had met after a long time apart due to a painful misunderstanding. They had finally gathered the courage to meet and address the rift that had fractured their once-close friendship. The close to empty coffee shop provided the space and time that would help them both to open their hearts and pour out their emotions.

There were a couple sitting in a corner and a man in the far end, deeply immersed in painting on a canvas. The aroma of freshly brewed coffee was lingering in the air that had the power to blend any broken hearts. As they walked in, they found a table in the centre of the café to be more comfortable. It looked like the meeting was just enough to resolve their differences. They shared a smile and felt the differences dissolving on its own. They both discussed about their lives during the past two years as to how their life shaped up for each other. As they touched upon many topics revolving around life, they embarked on a reflective conversation about the complexities of relationships and the enigmatic functioning of the human mind.

Kavya: (sipping her coffee, her eyes filled with contemplation) You know, Mark, it is peculiar thing to see how all relationships today are hanging on the edge of a ticking time bomb. I see these relationships are waiting for just one event that can shatter everything into pieces.

Mark: (nodding thoughtfully) I could not agree more, Kavya. It is like we have allowed our emotional threshold to fall so low that even a tiniest spark can ignite a wildfire in the relationship that can shatter all the happiness and tranquillity.

Kavya: Absolutely Mark. We have allowed our conscience and emotions to diminish to such an extent that we have become so much unaware that we are living in a state of profound unconsciousness. We have mastered the ability to conceal this lack of awareness by bolstering our ego and portraying it as overly confident of ourselves.

Mark: (his eyes revealing traces of regret) You know, Kavya, it is extremely disturbing how we abandon our authentic selves and adopted something more sluggish. It takes one event just one event to tear off this mask. You just toss a speck of dirt at someone; you will see their unconsciousness erupting to the surface.

Kavya: (acknowledging the unsettling truth) It is as if the ferocious animal within us eagerly awaits that solitary incident, the one that would reveal the animal to its full potential.

Mark: (nodding soberly, as if coming to terms with the complexities of human nature) It is strange that we are completely unaware of the beast that is always preventing us from achieving happiness.

Kavya: (smiling ruefully, a hint of irony in her tone) Mark, you are right. We all crave happiness, but it is almost ironic how, in pursuit of it, we often cause harm to the very thing we cherish the most – our happiness.

As Kavya and Mark continued their intense conversation, the flow was abruptly interrupted by the ringing of Kavya's mobile phone.

Kavya glanced at her phone to see who was calling, it was her mother trying to reach. She politely excused herself from Mark, assuring him that she will be back in a moment. She then made her way out of the coffee shop to answer her mother's call.

As Kavya left, Mark found himself slipping into a contemplative reverie. Memories of the day he made one of the toughest decisions of his life flooded back vividly. It was the day he walked away from his childhood home, leaving behind his beloved mother, the person with whom he had entrusted his deepest secrets. She was the one he shared all his life's ambitions with, relying on her to bridge the gap with his father, pushing her to seek his father's approval.

Mark had always felt more at ease communicating with his father indirectly through his mother, preferring to avoid direct confrontation to sidestep potential reprimand. He believed his mother possessed a unique ability to secure his father's acceptance effortlessly.

On that fateful day, Mark encountered a shock when his father had listed out a series of Mark's perceived mistakes. The mistakes stretching back to his earliest years. These list of allegation, Mark had assumed till date that it had the blessings of his father. But that belief had led to an unfortunate surprise.

Mark was puzzled by the timing of his father's decision to bombard allegations upon Mark. It occurred on the very moment when Mark demanded an explanation about a crucial family matter, on which he had been deliberately kept in the dark.

In a crucial moment, a realisation dawned upon Mark – all the allegations his father laid upon him were not his father's own interpretations. It became clear to Mark that his mother had never accurately conveyed Mark's true intentions. Instead, she had been delivering concise summaries of Mark's explanations, which had led to massive misunderstandings.

Mark attempted to clarify and present his side of the story, but the conversation spiralled into an ugly conflict. Mark was in no mood to accept any of the baseless allegations that his father hurled at him. These allegations escalated to such an extent that Mark felt his self-respect was under a brutal attack.

With no relief in sight, Mark made the immediate decision to leave. Departing from his family home signified more than just a physical departure. Mark was conscious of the sacrifices this choice involved. It meant he would no longer participate in any family celebrations, nor could he share his joys, sorrows, or achievements with them. The life he was leaving behind would not be the same for his spouse and children either.

As he prepared to move, he turned towards his mother for one last time and uttered, "Mom, what have you done to me? You know the whole truth. Please speak up for me, please."

She stayed there still and responded, "I have conveyed everything to your father".

Mark, "No, mom. You haven't. You haven't conveyed in detail."

On that fateful day, as Mark walked out with a heavy heart from the home where he had never truly belonged, along with his spouse and children, he silently whispered to himself, "I shall never, ever step into the same path where I lost my self-respect".

His eyes brimmed with tears, but as Mark noticed Kavya returning to the café, he swiftly brushed them away and mustered a warm, welcoming smile, ready to greet her after her conversation with her mother.

As Kavya made her way back to their table, her eyes were drawn to the artist seated in the far corner, a triumphant smile illuminating his face. It looked like he had completed his masterpiece. Curiosity tugging at her, she thought to take a moment to appreciate his work.

Upon closer observation, Kavya was captivated by the artwork. It was a canvas filled with vibrant masks, each one in distinct colours. She could not help but wonder about the message the artist intended to convey with this unusual piece.

Then, her gaze fell upon a seemingly empty space with the composition, she believed there was more to this canvas than that met the eye. Stepping closer for a better look, she discerned the hidden layers of meaning.

"It's not an empty space," she whispered to herself, her eyes tracking the intricate details. As she continued to study the artwork, she noticed a human face hidden in between the masks with tears streaming from its eyes and as her gaze descended, she saw a mask, once a part of that face, now falling away.

9

Smart As Owl!

The tiger, his stomach growling with hunger, stood still, eyes fixed on the horizon, ears perked up, ready to spring into action at the slightest sight of its prey.

On the outside, he appeared calm and complacent, but inside, his hunger gnawed at him, growing with each passing moment. To an onlooker, it might seem like the tiger was idly wasting time, but, he had no choice but to wait patiently. He had traversed a long distance in search of his elusive meal, and conserving his energy was crucial for the imminent hunt.

Perched on a nearby tree, an observant owl noticed the motionless tiger. The wise owl, puzzled by the tiger's inactivity, wondered how someone could waste precious time like this. The owl observed the tiger for some more time, but his wise mind couldn't endure the sight any longer. He decided to offer some words of motivation, illuminating from his treasured wisdom!

Owl called out to the tiger, "Hey there, my friend! Do you need any assistance? You seem a bit unmotivated and lost."

The tiger's hunger was reaching an unbearable intensity and he was getting a bit impatient. Yet, he responded keeping his composure, "I am just waiting for the right moment, that's all."

Owl with sagely wisdom, "Waiting is fine, but remember, time lost can never be regained. You need to stay active."

The tiger's hunger intensified, making it even more restless.

The owl continued sharing his pearls of wisdom to the tiger. He points towards distant animals, "Look over there. See those animals? They are busy grazing and staying active. You could learn from them.

The tiger growing more impatient, "Those animals live on a farm, and everything's handed to them. I'm a hunter; life is not the same for me!

The owl instantly replied, "It's all in your mindset, my friend. Maybe try doing what they are doing instead of waiting and wasting your time.

The tiger, irritated by the owl's persistence, chose not to respond. His focus remained on the distant horizon, where its potential prey might appear.

As time passed, the owl's incessant lecturing tried the tiger's patience. For a moment, he felt like lashing out at the owl, but he resisted. He understood that giving in to impatience could not only sour his relationship with the owl but also jeopardize his chances of a successful hunt.

Finally, after what felt like an eternity, the tiger's patience was rewarded. In the far distance, he spotted the signs of his prey. His sharp, focused eyes locked onto the target. The sharp-eyed owl could not realise this event. He was still deeply engrossed in his lecture.

Without wasting a second, the tiger sprang into action, sprinting toward his target with unwavering focus and determination. He knew that its patience and single-mindedness were about to pay off.

The owl observed the sudden shift in the tiger's vigour and efforts. He felt a sense of pride in its ability to transform the tiger from a state of apparent laziness into one of enthusiasm.

The owl wore a content look on his face. He was ultimately convinced that that there is no one smart on the earth is as SMART AS OWL!

10

Badminton Buddies

"Hey… Sorry buddies… I am late today", Sidharth walked in apologizing to his badminton buddies.

"I had to tackle a last-minute issue that came up when I was just about to wind up the day's work."

"It's okay, Sidharth. We had an extra moment to play for ourselves", chuckled Aayushi and missed the shuttle flying her way. Clement was generous enough to serve again to accommodate her miss while talking to Sidharth. Clement walked towards Sidharth, gave a high-five to Sidharth, and handed his racket to him.

"Go ahead, buddy. We played enough today. And yeah… we all could taste some victory today while you were still on the way."

Aayushi laughed out loud at the comment by Clement. Riyaz and Smita joined her and laughed too. They all know what Clement meant. Sidharth gave a graceful smile, grabbed the opportunity, and jumped straight into action.

Sidharth is known as a perfectionist in his circle. As per him, there is nothing called a small or big occasion. He always feels all actions are to be given equal attention. This approach to life enables him to accomplish anything with ease. Even in the game, he is the ace most of the time. That was the reason for the laugh when Clement mentioned the group could taste some victory. It is always Sidharth who makes the winning shot at the end.

Sometimes he gets mocked for his perfection. He describes when you can do something right at the first moment with the same effort of doing it wrong and correcting it later. That is an utter waste of time and resources. His inspiring words are, 'How you do anything is how you do everything".

Sidharth grabbed the opportunity to hold the racket instantly and jumped into action straight away. Taking aces, with most of his delivery. There was a sudden spurt in energy as the game shifted to an even faster pace.

They had to pause occasionally to give way to the vehicles entering the lane. That was a hindrance every time they played. They were used to it. They cannot complain. After all, it's they who have converted the public road into a private game arena. They have no other option but to pause their game.

They all sat near a vacant plot on a long stone that looked like a bench to have a closing chat before they walked into their own dens and settled down with their respective families for the rest of the day. The owner of the plot might have brought these stones to put a wired fence. But was too lazy or held up elsewhere to ignore this task. The stone could accommodate only three people. The rest of the two had to stand. Today, Sidharth and Smita stood while Riyaz, Aayushi and Clement sat on the stone bench.

The conversation went all the way from their day at the office to the welfare activities in the community. While the conversation was at the intersection of too many interesting topics, Smita exclaimed interrupting the conversation abruptly. This is not a pattern or nature of anyone in this group to divert a topic in discussion. They all feel complete only when nothing is left to talk about it. They all love to go as deep as possible into any subject they start. But the unusual happened today. Everyone looked at her to express herself.

Smita, "Hey... guys... I have got an idea!"

She continued, "Look over there", she looked beyond the folks sitting on the stone. Sidharth looked past them too. Clement, Aayushi and Riyaz turned around to see what Smita was showing. Everyone turned back to Smita curiously to hear more from her.

"Look at the debris in this vacant plot. Why don't we clean this up and make it our own private badminton court?"

The idea intrigued everyone, and they exchanged glances filled with excitement. A private badminton court would be a dream come true for their group. They would not have to worry about pausing the game for passing vehicles anymore, and they could play whenever they wanted without any interruptions.

Clement was the first to respond, "That's actually a brilliant idea, Smita! We could clear up the debris, level the ground a bit, and even put up a makeshift net. It won't be a professional court, but it'll be our very own space to play without any disturbances."

Aayushi added, "And we can bring some old rugs or mats to mark the boundaries. It doesn't have to be perfect, but it'll be our little badminton haven."

Riyaz nodded in agreement, "It's worth a shot. We all love playing and having our private court would be so much fun. We could even invite a few more friends to join us occasionally."

Sidharth, who was known for his practicality, chimed in, "Let's not get too carried away with the idea, but I think it's definitely worth trying. We can start by cleaning up the area and seeing how it goes. If it works out well, we can think about making some improvements."

Smita beamed with enthusiasm, "Great! Let us plan a day when we can all get together and start the cleanup. I will also find the owner of this plot and check if they are okay with us using it for a small badminton court. I don't think they would mind, considering it's just a vacant space." She eventually forgot it.

Over the next few days, the group put their plan into action. They coordinated with each other to bring the required tools for cleaning, like brooms, shovels, and trash bags. They worked tirelessly, removing the debris, and levelling the ground as much as possible. It was arduous work, but the excitement of having their private badminton court motivated them to keep going.

The cleaning of the ground has almost ended. The friends were busy tidying up the place while Aayushi felt like someone was staring at her from back. Her woman intuition proved right again. This man was standing in the aisle of the vacant plot looking at the busy people. He was not staring at Aayushi as she felt so. He looked amused and looked interested in the activities of the team.

Aayushi looked straight into the stranger's eyes and felt herself smiling to herself and warmth. She walked forward to the stranger.

"Hello, I am Aayushi."

The stranger replied, "Hi, Aayushi! Nice to meet you. I am Praveen." Praveen continued, "I was passing by the place and saw you folks cleaning up this place."

Aayushi replied with enthusiasm, "We just removed the debris and tidied this plot and converted this place as a makeshift badminton court to play badminton during the evenings.," She told, "All these days we were playing on the street that was too intriguing and a disturbance to the passing vehicles and us. Once this place is done, we shall have an uninterrupted game session all evening."

Praveen said it is a brilliant idea, "I appreciate this initiative. Can I too join to play with you, people. I am all set to dirty my hands too along with you in bringing up the court." He further added, "I live three houses from here at 203." Aayushi spurted, "That's where my friend Pallavi lives." Praveen smiled back, "Yes. It's such a coincidence. I am her husband."

Aayushi, "That is wonderful to know Praveen. Really glad to meet my friend's husband. I have been insisting, she join us sometimes. But she is usually busy at this hour at her boutique." Praveen nodded in agreement.

Praveen, "I get to see her only after 9:00 PM every day. You rightly mentioned. She is usually busy at this time of the day."

Getting back to the conversation about the court, Aayushi welcomed his offer. But she hesitated and said, "I need to consult with my other partners. We had pooled-in money to shift the debris and clean up this place."

Praveen without any hesitation offered instantly to contribute to the expenses. His offer turned her hesitation into a grin.

Aayushi called out for Clement, Smita, Sidharth and Riyaz. He guys... come one here. Meet Praveen. Praveen is keen to join us in our makeshift badminton court project! He has offered to share the expenses. I just learnt that my close friend Pallavi is his spouse.

They all were happy to meet Praveen and appreciated his offer to join them in their project! He shook hands with Clement, Smita, Sidharth and Riyaz. The whole team gladly accepted his friendship and his offer to share the expenses.

Praveen instantly jumped into action and joined the craze. The cleaning went on for the next two days. They paused their games till then.

Once they completed the cleaning, they brought old rugs and marked the boundaries. They decided to use makeshift markers for the net and practiced playing to see how it felt. The joy of playing on their own court, even if it was simple, was incomparable. They knew they had made the right decision. Their happiness doubled knowing eventually that Praveen is of their own mindset. Praveen was an amicable chap and jelled with the team with ease.

As word spread among their friends and the community, more people showed interest in joining their badminton games. The group gladly welcomed them, and the court became a gathering spot for badminton enthusiasts. They made new friends, and the bond among the existing members grew even stronger.

With time, they made improvements to the court, like adding some lighting for evening matches and painting lines for a more professional look. Though it was a humble setup, it held a special place in their hearts.

Their private badminton court became a symbol of friendship, unity, and the joy of pursuing a common passion. It was a testament to their determination to make the most out of any situation and turn a simple vacant plot into something special. Every time they stepped onto that court, all of them were reminded of the power of their collective efforts and the beauty of sharing simple pleasures with good friends. And so, the Badminton Buddies' private court continued to be a cherished part of their lives.

They thoroughly enjoyed playing uninterrupted games every evening. They had occasional visitors who played one or two sets of games. Their circle of friends was expanding. They laid down seats at a corner of the court to relax in between the game which also served as served as an intellectual corner after the game time.

Sidharth continued to hold the status of ace player. Clement, Aayushi, Riyaz and Smita tried their best to beat him. Praveen too joined them in the struggle to beat Sidharth. They played countless matches. They also improved their skills by observing Sidharth's talent in playing with ease.

One evening after the game, Riyaz remembered that they were to find out the owner of the plot. He turned to Smita, "Smita, did you find out the owner of this plot. It's not fair on our part otherwise."

Smita gave an apologetic look, "Riyaz, I totally forgot about it. It slipped off my mind, amidst the excitement of getting our own place to play."

Smita, Clement and Aayushi looked at each other with concern. Smita apologetically offered to find out in the next few days. They all nodded at each other.

Sidharth and Praveen did not join the game this evening. Sidharth had a late evening meeting and texted the Badminton Buddies group that he will not be joining for the game this evening. Praveen had texted too that he is caught up with work with an assurance to join the post-game conversation.

Aayushi said, "Maybe the owner of this plot does not live here. Else, he might have already had the information."

Clement agreed with Aayushi and added, "Probably the owner might have known this and has silently allowed us to use the place until he or she plans to construct a house here."

Just then Praveen arrived and got worried looking at the pensive faces of his friends. "What makes my good friends so immersed in some serious thoughts today? Hope you enjoyed the game with some good wins without Sidharth." He smiled. All the others returned an uncomfortable smile.

Praveen insisted, "Come on folks, enlighten me. Allow me too to immerse in your serious though."

Smita broke the silence, "Praveen, actually when we got the thought of cleaning up this place to make it our private court, I had volunteered to find out the owner of this plot and seek their permission to play here until they decide to construct their home." She continued, I somehow missed out on doing so in the whole excitement of getting our private space. I should have been thoughtful about this. What if, suddenly the owner turns up here and asks us to vacate at once."

Praveen threw back a relaxed look, "Oh well! Now, I see your concern. Never mind, the owner of this plot is not planning to construct a house until his wife's boutique business stabilizes. Not before two more years"

Aayushi was the first one to react, "What? Are you going to surprise us once again? Are you the owner of this plot?" Clement, Smita and Riyaz joined along with Aayushi's question to Praveen.

"Yes, Aayushi. The other day I walked here to question you folks for encroaching on my property. Eventually, I found out that you did not encroach, but were only making this a better place, a place to play and have meaningful meetings. I used to commute five kilometers every day to play in a club. Looking at your company, I thought it would be a better idea to join you people and save my travelling time to the club and I can play the same game here.", he concluded with a sheepish smile.

All others were dumbstruck. Praveen continued, "I am glad that not only I found a place to play, that too on my own plot, I am also so happy that I found a good friendship in you all that is too close to my rented house. Technically, we have two more years to play in this plot. What next? Yes. After two years, let's start again in search of the next owner who does not have a plan to construct a house for two years and is also an avid badminton enthusiast."

Upon listening to Praveen's long speech, Smita breathed a long sigh of relief. Clement, Riyaz and Aayushi jumped and unanimously exclaimed, "We have a story to tell Sidharth tomorrow. He really missed it today. Thank you, Praveen! You had been such a nice guy and we must reprimand you with a treat for keeping us in suspense all these days."

11

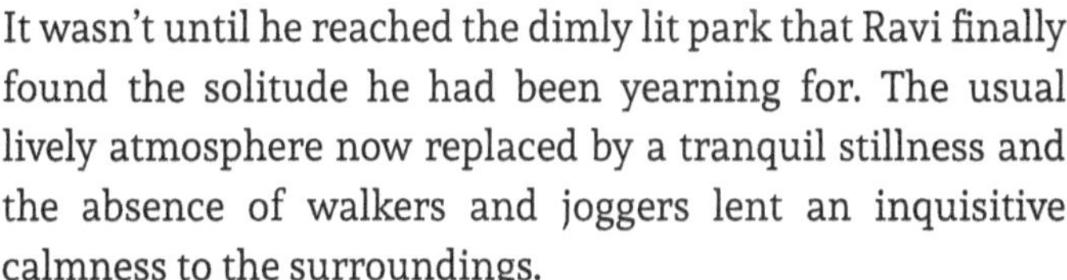

It wasn't until he reached the dimly lit park that Ravi finally found the solitude he had been yearning for. The usual lively atmosphere now replaced by a tranquil stillness and the absence of walkers and joggers lent an inquisitive calmness to the surroundings.

As he made his way deeper into the park, Ravi couldn't help but notice there were couples scattered here and there taking refuge under the cover of darkness. They were sitting and lying down in various asanas that are not taught in any yoga schools. Each couple had invented their own asanas, their bodies entwined as they sought to discreetly explore what lay hidden beneath their partner's costumes. A few others had already shed it away partially revealing glimpses of skin in the dim light of the park. Some whispered secrets in each other's ears, their laughter mingling with the rustle of leaves overhead. A few exchanged coy glances, their fingers tracing patterns along the curves of their partner's skin.

For a moment, Ravi allowed himself to linger on the edge of their world, attracted by the sense of closeness and connection that seemed to bind them together. But then, shaking away his head, he dismissed the thought and continued his way.

Finding a secluded spot, Ravi sank down onto a bench, the turmoil of his emotions finally catching up to him. His breath swelled due to the vigorous walk he had undertaken to clear his mind. But his mind was unsettled and was trying to walk back the five kilometers he had just crossed.

ᐅᐅᐅ

In the dimly lit car that took an avatar of makeshift bar, a group of friends gathered to unwind during the weekend. The evening starts buzzing with chatter and the clinking of glasses.

As the night unfolded and the drinks flowed freely, the mood of the group grew increasingly sour. "You know what your problem is, Ravi?" Ashish spoke, his words cutting through Ravi's head like a laser. "You are always running away from your mistakes, pretending like they never happened. But they are still there, lurking in the shadows, waiting to catch up with you." Ravi instantly identified; he is the prey of the day. Now, one by one, each of his friends would take their turn to prickle the wound with ruthless precision. This was a usual cruel game they played once they got high on alcohol with a determination to bring each other down from their level.

The same pattern repeated itself week after Week. One member of the group would become the focus of collective scorn. The target would be made feel small and insignificant, forced to plead guilty as an outcome of their relentless criticism.

Ravi sat among this group of friends, feeling the burden of their negativity pressing down on him like a heavy boulder. He stayed away from this cruel game, instead choosing to share stories of kindness and compassion, of triumphs and successes. He tried to lift the spirits of his friends, to remind them that there was more to life than tearing each other apart.

But his efforts were unsuccessful. The others were too far gone, too entrenched in their cycle of negativity to visualize the harm they were causing. And as the weeks passed, Ravi found himself growing increasingly disillusioned with the group.

Ashish continued with his relentless interrogation. Satish and Kumar joined the bandwagon. He drew up the same topic for the nth time over the years of their friendship, with an intention to chip away Ravi's confidence until he was left feeling exposed and vulnerable. And each time they succeeded; it left a trail of broken spirits in the group.

Deep down, Ravi longed to spread positivity and lift others up, but it seemed like an impossible task amid such negativity. He knew he could not change the entire group's behaviour, but he could not stand by and watch them continue to tear each other apart either.

For years now, he had endured their constant criticisms, their relentless reminders of his past failures. But tonight, something inside him shattered.

"You all are bastards", Ravi's voice cut through the chaos, sharp and stern. With those words, he opened the door and stepped out of the car swiftly and started to walk away from them never to return. He did not wait for a response, did not want to see the looks of shock or confusion on their faces.

As he continued walking, Ravi felt a surge of adrenaline streaming through his veins. It was as if a heavy weight had just been lifted from his chest, leaving him feeling lighter and freer than he had in ages.

But even as he relished his newfound freedom, Ravi could not shake the nagging feeling of doubt that lingered in the back of his mind. Had he done the right thing by walking away? Would he regret cutting ties with his friends, no matter how toxic they had become?

ᗅᗅᗅ

Closing his eyes, Ravi took a deep breath, wanting to find peace amidst the chaos of his thoughts. Slowly, he brought his attention back to the present moment, focusing on the sensation of the cool night air against his skin and the rhythmic sound of his own heartbeat.

Ravi made the ultimate decision. He would not let the negativity of his past hold him back any longer. He would surround himself with positive influences, with people who believed in him and his dreams.

For the first time, he dared to believe that a brighter future was possible, he trusted his capability to achieve great things.

And as the first light of dawn crept over the horizon, Ravi knew that he was ready to spread his wings and soar, unfettered by the shadows of his past.

He was good to FLY!

12

Pretty Woman Walking Down the Street

It was already 8:30 PM, and Richa wound up her work with a sense of dejection. She had not made any closure today. Selling course packages to the parents of middle school children was a challenge. She looked at Tania, who sighed and signalled Richa to leave. Some parents must have given time at this hour for the demo. Richa signalled back that she would secure her dinner at the PG and left the office.

As Richa reached the Brookfield bus stand to cross the busy road, her phone buzzed. It was Suman calling. Her face lit up instantly upon seeing Suman's name. She picked up the call on the first ring.

"Hey, honey! Wassup. Glad you called me now. I just left the office. I have not seen you at your desk since evening."

"Yes, baby, I had left to meet a client. I wish you had joined too. That was a good call. I hope I will close this sale. I think I will catch up with your number this month," Suman spoke with enthusiasm.

"Yes, dear. That's the hope. But I am not sure how I will make it. We have just five days left to close this month.

Today was a disappointing day. I could not even get close to securing an appointment."

"Oh! Some days are indeed frustrating," he continued. "Baby, you know what? My roomie has gone home. He's not going to be back till Sunday," his voice titillating.

Richa blushed with anticipation of what's coming next. She walked across the road, clutching her phone closer to her ear so as not to miss any excitement coming through the earpiece amidst the buzzing traffic.

"Wow! What a terrific news, honey. You are going to be alone tonight," continued blushing.

"Yes. Yes, honey. Very much. But not alone. My darling is going to come over," Suman said with an inviting tone. The excitement rose higher, and she could feel the stiffness in her nipples. She imagined Suman cupping her bosoms from behind.

"You know, honey, I have been hungry for so many nights, waiting for this moment. Tonight, I'm going to turn into a beast and feast on you."

Suman chuckled, "Oh really? I'm glad to be your feast. But honey, spare my hands. They are going to be busy upscaling my beast's feast."

She continued walking amidst the animated conversation with Suman when something made her stumble suddenly. A furious bike was approaching her. Richa managed to walk past the bike.

As she continued her romantic conversation with Suman, she stumbled again. Another speeding bike swished in front of her. Richa stood there, sandwiched between the two bikes, smiling with anticipation building for the evening ahead, which promised an exciting night full of action. She didn't want to waste a single moment and started longing for that moment in bed with Suman.

"I can't wait anymore, honey. I am coming over right away," she said, the urgency in her voice reaching Suman instantly.

"Yes, honey. Can't wait anymore. Come soon," Suman replied.

Next, Richa texted Tania, 'Tanu, my plan changed, I am heading out to Suman's place. I will see you at the PG tomorrow morning. Please manage your dinner na. I am in a hurry, dear.'

ᎮᎮᎮ

Suman started his KTM 390 Duke and, before getting on the move, dialled Richa's number. She picked up his call on the first ring. He began moving his bike, placing his phone on his shoulder blade, and lifting his shoulder to bring the phone closer to his ear. He slightly tilted his head to the right to get a better grip on the phone, trying to comfortably talk while riding. He navigated through the busy road, eager to reach home quickly.

His excitement grew as Richa teased, "You know, honey, I have been hungry for so many nights, waiting for this moment. Tonight, I'm going to turn into a beast and feast on you."

Suman chuckled, "Oh really? I'm glad to be your feast. But honey, spare my hands. They are going to be busy upscaling my beast's feast."

It was just then, out of nowhere, this woman, engrossed in her phone conversation, walked right into his path. He swerved, narrowly missing her.

As he looked to the side, he saw another bike speeding besides her. She was sandwiched between his bike and the other one. She had no sign of understanding the peril she was in. As he passed by her, he took out his phone from its saddle and glanced back, half-expecting her to be shaken. Instead, she stood there, still talking, and smiling. How could she not realize how close she came to getting hit?

He had no time deal with this nonsense right now. Richa might reach his home any moment. He put his phone back to its saddle as Richa continued, "I can't wait anymore, honey. I am coming over right away," she said, the urgency in her voice reaching him instantly.

"Yes, honey. Can't wait anymore. Come soon," he replied.

He sped towards his flat, anticipation building under his pants with each passing second at the thought of relishing her body through the night.

ÞÞÞ

Santosh had accepted two deliveries at the same time, one from Zomato and another from Swiggy. This strategy made it easier for him to make a quick money, as these apps allow only one delivery at a time. He picked up his first delivery from Mayura Sagar and headed towards TN81 for the next pick up.

As he rode his Honda Activa, his phone rang. It was his mother calling. He picked up the call, but then his other phone rang. He asked his mother to hold on and placed the phone under his thigh, retrieving the other phone from the left pocket of his pants. It was a customer's call. He quickly assured the customer that he was on his way to deliver their order, then placed the phone back in his left pocket and resumed his conversation with his mother.

The other phone rang again. Santosh once more put the phone under his thigh to deal with the call. It was his friend Madhu. He excused himself and picked up the first phone, telling his mother he would call her back before placing it in his right pocket. He continued his conversation with

Madhu while speeding towards TN81.

Suddenly, he noticed a pretty woman walking in the middle of the road, engrossed in her phone. Santosh swerved across her to secure his position to pass first. As he passed her, he turned to steal a quick glance at her beauty. He completely forgot about Madhu, who was still on the other end of the call.

Madhu's voice became louder, yelling through the phone to regain Santosh's attention.

ᗡᗡᗡ

Driving a bus in this city is no easy task. But for Venkatesh, it had always been a cakewalk. He had spent a respectable number of years with BMTC. He possessed the rare knack of gliding the bus sideways tactfully, with the enchanting feeling that he was the next champion of a Japanese Drift, startling other vehicles into a jolting halt and passing through them like a hot knife cutting through butter.

As he was crossing the Graphite India bus stand, his phone rang. It was his wife on the other side. Immersed in the conversation, he continued to drive at top speed, pushing away all the other vehicles that hindered his path. He was reaching Brookfield bus stand and just then a rider on KTM cut past in front of him, a rare event he came across. No one dared to cut through a BMTC bus; that was the unsaid norm for ages.

Agitated, Venkatesh then spotted a hep-looking woman right in front of the bus. He realised that the KTM rider had swerved to avoid hitting her, and a Honda Activa was on the other side of her. The lady was sandwiched between the two bikes. Venkatesh slammed his foot on the brake pedal, knowing the bus wouldn't stop easily at such speed.

He finally managed to bring the bus to a screeching halt, nearly throwing out all the passengers through the windshield.

ᖰᖰᖰ

Richa crossed the road unscathed, her excitement building as she looked forward to spending the night with Suman.

Suman arrived home early, eagerly anticipating a wonderful night with Richa.

Santosh felt fortunate to have completed his two deliveries successfully, his mind mulling over the beautiful women he just saw.

Venkatesh continued his conversation with his wife, halting the bus 100 meters away from the Brookfield bus stand as usual.

Yes. I know all these. I was there, a silent witness to the avoided massacre – the near misses of the girl, the two bikers and the bus driver. I was there with all of them at the same time.

I take the blame every time a catastrophe happens.

But why? Why do they blame me? I just brought them all so close to each other.

Why am I not still a marvellous pretty thing?

9 7 9 8 8 8 9 5 4 4 7 8 4 0